For Odette, who loves
B. B.

For Miss Dove and Miss McLeod
K. M. D.

Text copyright © 2014 by Bonny Becker
Illustrations copyright © 2014 by Kady MacDonald Denton

First edition 2014

Library of Congress Catalog Card Number 2013952827
ISBN 978-0-7636-4924-1

14 15 16 17 18 19 WKT 10 9 8 7 6 5 4 3 2 1

Printed in Shenzhen, Guangdong, China

This book was typeset in New Baskerville.
The illustrations were done in watercolor, ink, and gouache.

Candlewick Press
99 Dover Street
Somerville, Massachusetts 02144

visit us at www.candlewick.com

A Library Book for Bear

Bonny Becker

illustrated by

Kady MacDonald Denton

CANDLEWICK PRESS

Bear had never been to the library.
He had seven very nice books at home:
three about kings and queens, three about honeybees,
and one about pickles.
Bear was quite sure he had
all the books he would ever need.

One morning, Bear heard a tap, tap, tapping on his door.

When he opened the door, there was Mouse, small and gray and bright-eyed.

"We are off!" exclaimed Mouse with a happy wag of his whiskers.

Bear frowned. He had agreed to go with Mouse to the library, but now

he was quite sure it was a dreadful mistake.

"Completely unnecessary," Bear announced. "I have all the books I need right here."

"Oh, there are many delightful books in the library," Mouse assured him.

"Hmmph!" Bear grumbled, but he *had* promised.

So he buckled up his red roller skates and stepped outside, grabbing a basket for the books.

Bear skated and Mouse rode in the basket to the library, the wind rippling nicely through their fur.

But when they got to the library, Bear didn't like how big it looked.

"There are far too many books in there," he protested. "Most excessive!"

"Oh, no. It's quite exciting," Mouse said, leading Bear through the tall doors.

In the library were more books than Bear had ever thought there could be.

He quickly found a tucked-away corner. But even here, there were lots and

lots of books.

"Hmmph! Terribly extravagant!" Bear's voice was a little loud.

"I shall find you the perfect one," Mouse said quietly in his library voice.

"One about pickles," commanded Bear. After all, he only had one of those.

But Mouse had whisked away.

Mouse came back with a thick green book. Bear opened it.

"Rocket ships! Ridiculous!" Bear's voice was getting louder. "A good
  book about pickles is all I require!"

"Remember—quiet in the library," murmured Mouse as he scurried off.

He soon returned with a tall yellow book.

"I am not interested in wooden canoes!"

Bear's voice was even louder.

"Quiet voices in the library," Mouse reminded him.

"My voice is always quiet," Bear shouted.
"I will find my own book. I can assure you that pickles are quite interesting!"

Mouse didn't look so sure. But Bear quickly spotted a blue book with
a pickle on the spine, and Mouse sprang up the shelf to get it for him.

Inside were pictures of pickles. The pickles had little fairy wings.

They were dancing with petunias.

"NO DANCING PICKLES!" Bear roared.

"SHHHHHHHH!" said a voice.

Bear peeked around a bookshelf.

There sat a librarian with a cluster of youngsters gathered around her. The librarian smiled, but a mother squirrel squished an angry finger against her lips, and an old raccoon said sternly, "Quiet in the library."

Bear turned back with a huffy sniff. "I know when I'm not wanted," he told Mouse. "I want to go home." "Surely, at least one book—" Mouse began.

But Bear cut him off: "I have all the books I need."

He looked quite certain.

"Then, we are off," said Mouse, but his whiskers didn't wag this time.

Bear stood stock-still. He was listening carefully to a
voice on the other side of the bookshelf.

"So the Very Brave Bear began to inch his way toward the treasure chest . . ."
the voice was saying.

"I'm ready—" began Mouse.

"SHHHHHHHHH!" exclaimed Bear.

"It's just getting to the good part!"

"But, you said—"

"QUIET VOICES IN THE LIBRARY!"

Bear bellowed.

This time the librarian got up and looked around the bookshelf at Bear.

Bear stood very still and quiet, as if he had been still and quiet all along.

"Would you like to join story time?" the librarian asked.

Bear glanced at Mouse.

"We'd love to have you," said the librarian.

Bear and Mouse scooted around the shelf and found two empty chairs.

The librarian began to read again.

"Bear lifted the lid to the treasure chest, and inside . . ."

The librarian paused. Mouse and Bear strained forward.

"*Inside,*" she said, "*was a mound of pickle slices. And each shining slice was made of diamonds and gold! And everyone shouted, 'Hooray for the Very Brave Bear!'*"
And then she said, "*The End.*"

Bear stared dreamily into space for a moment. Then he looked over at Mouse and announced, "As I said, pickles are most interesting."

"Indeed," said Mouse.

Later, Mouse rode in the basket with seven new books. There were two about wooden canoes, two about rocket ships, two about teapots . . .

and one called *The Very Brave Bear and the Treasure of Pickle Island,*
which Bear read to Mouse that very same day.